Jade
the Disco
Fairy

To Emma and Kate Savage
with lots of love.

Special thanks to Sue Mongredien

ISBN-10: 0-545-10616-8
ISBN-13: 978-0-545-10616-0

12 11 10 9 8 7 6 5 4 3 2 1   9 10 11 12 13/0

Printed in the U.S.A.

First Scholastic Printing, May 2009

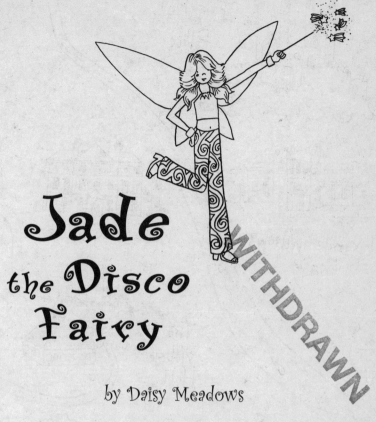

Jade
the Disco
Fairy

by Daisy Meadows

SCHOLASTIC INC.

New York Toronto London Auckland Sydney
Mexico City New Delhi Hong Kong Buenos Aires

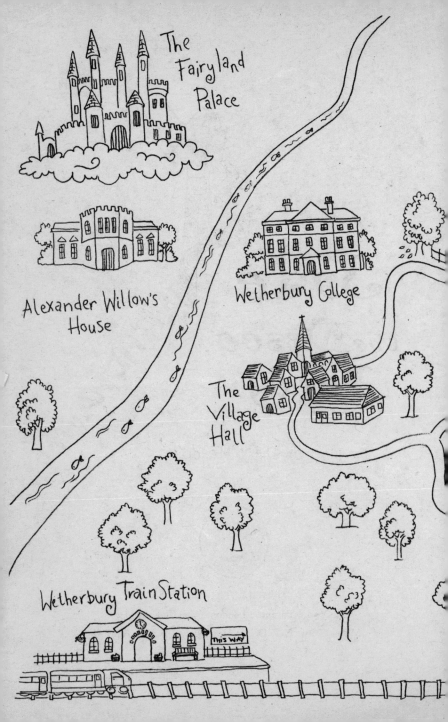

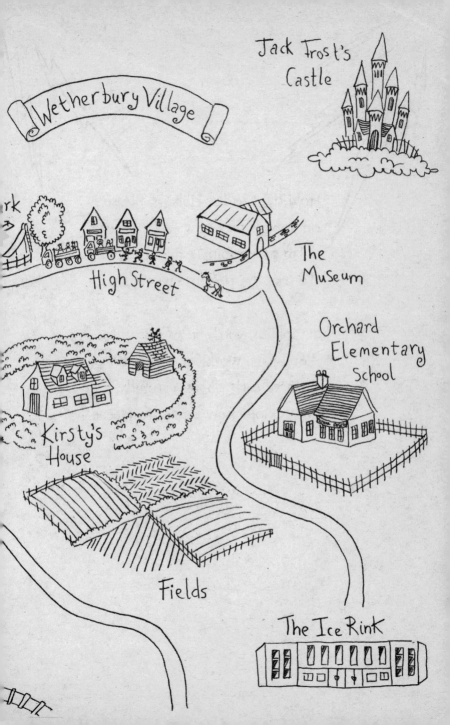

Hold tight to the ribbons, please.
You goblins may now feel a breeze.
I'm summoning a hurricane
To take the ribbons away again.

But, goblins, you'll be swept up too,
For I have work for you to do.
Guard each ribbon carefully,
By using your new power to freeze.

Contents

Girls Go Dancing

"Strike!" cheered Kirsty Tate, as Rachel's ball sent all ten pins flying at the end of the bowling lane.

"Hooray!" Rachel cried in delight.

"That's your third strike today!" Kirsty's dad said, smiling. "Good job, Rachel."

"And it looks like you won the game, too!" Mrs. Tate added, gazing up at the electronic scoreboard.

The girls went to see. Sure enough, flashing green letters spelled out 'RACHEL WINS' on the screen.

"Yay!" Rachel said. "I'm having the best vacation ever — and it's only just begun!"

She and Kirsty grinned at each other.
Rachel was staying with Kirsty's family
for their school break, and the two girls
always had exciting adventures whenever
they were together. *Fairy* adventures!
This time was no different. Only
yesterday, they'd met the seven Dance
Fairies, who'd asked for their help. The
girls had said yes right away.
They loved helping the
fairies!

"Well, girls," Mr. Tate
said as the scoreboard
flashed 'GAME OVER.'
"It's time to take off
your bowling shoes and
put on your dancing shoes.
You have the school disco
tonight, remember?"

"I can't wait," Kirsty said eagerly, turning to her friend. "Rachel and I love dancing, don't we?"

Rachel nodded, knowing Kirsty was thinking about the Dance Fairies. "Definitely," she replied. "Come on, let's go!"

Once they were back at the Tates' house, the girls got changed in Kirsty's bedroom. Rachel was wearing a pretty purple party dress, and Kirsty picked out a pink sparkly top and a pair of black pants. "I can't wait to see all your friends again," Rachel said, brushing her hair in front of the mirror.

"It'll be great to dance with them tonight."

Kirsty went over to check that her door was closed properly. "We might even get to see another one of the Dance Fairies, too!" she added in a low voice.

"I hope so," Rachel said eagerly. Yesterday, she and Kirsty had met all seven Dance Fairies and been magically whisked away to Fairyland. There, they'd learned that the Dance Fairies' magical ribbons had been stolen by Jack Frost.

The fairies had explained that the ribbons made it so that dancing went smoothly and was fun for everyone in Fairyland and in the human world, too.

Jack Frost had stolen the ribbons
because he wanted his goblins
to be able to dance well at
a party he was throwing.

Together with the
Dance Fairies and the
fairy king and queen,
Rachel and Kirsty had
gone to Jack Frost's ice
castle to try and get the
ribbons back.

But when he saw them
coming, sneaky Jack Frost had
sent all the ribbons into the
human world, with a goblin
to guard each one.
Yesterday, the girls had
helped Bethany the Ballet Fairy
find the goblin with her ballet ribbon.

They'd gotten the ribbon back, but they'd been shocked to discover that Jack Frost had given his goblins a new magical power. While they had the ribbons, the goblins could freeze anything just by touching it!

Kirsty picked up a barrette and began fastening it in her hair. Then she stopped and looked at Rachel with a worried expression. "I just thought of something," she said. "What if the school disco is all messed up because the disco ribbon is still missing?"

Rachel bit her lip. "I hope not," she said. "It would be awful if the school dance was

ruined. We'll have to look for the goblin
and hope that we can get the magic
ribbon back to Jade the Disco Fairy
before anything goes wrong."

Kirsty nodded. "I don't like the thought
of meeting another goblin who can
freeze us." She shivered. "But we have to
try and save the disco!"

Groovy Goblin

"See you later, girls," Mrs. Tate said, as she dropped Kirsty and Rachel off at the school. "Have fun!"

"Bye, Mom! We will," Kirsty replied, waving. She and Rachel walked toward the doors. They could hear music pounding as they approached. The girls exchanged hopeful looks.

"The disco seems to be going all right so far," Rachel said optimistically. "I mean, the music's playing, so it hasn't been cancelled or anything. . . ."

Kirsty pushed open the doors. "Oh, and look!" she cried happily. "The gym is all decorated. It's so pretty!"

Rachel and Kirsty gazed around the large

gymnasium. Balloons and streamers were pinned high in the corners of the room, and colored lights flashed on the dance floor. Above their heads, sparkling mirror balls hung from the ceiling, sending tiny rainbow reflections spinning all around the room.

"Wow!" said Rachel. "It looks great . . . but no one is dancing."

The girls looked at the empty dance floor. There were clusters of girls and boys all around the room, but nobody was actually dancing to the music.

"Maybe it's a good thing," Kirsty said in a low voice. "Since the disco ribbon isn't on Jade's wand, everyone's dancing would probably be really bad, anyway."

Rachel was about
to agree when the
song changed and
two adults took to
the dance floor,
with self-
conscious smiles
on their faces.

Kirsty's eyes widened. "It's Mr. Collins
and Mrs. Adams!" she said.

"It looks like they're trying to get the
disco started," Rachel added, watching
as the teachers began to dance. Mr.
Collins started shaking his hips to the
music, but somehow this caused his legs
to go in opposite directions. He slipped
and went flying into Mrs. Adams! Mrs.
Adams wobbled as he crashed into her,

and her arms flailed as she tried to keep
her balance.

Kirsty looked at Rachel. "Oh no," she
said. "I was afraid this would happen!"

Rachel nodded. "We really need the
disco ribbon!"

People around the room were giggling
because the two teachers seemed to be
getting worse by the second. Mrs. Adams

trampled Mr. Collins' toes, then he
knocked her glasses off as he attempted
to do a groovy finger-pointing move!

"They are *so* bad." A girl standing near
Kirsty and Rachel giggled to her friends.
"I can't believe they're such awful
dancers!"

"Come on, *we* can't be any
worse than they are," one of
her friends replied. "Let's go
and show them how it's done!"

The group of girls edged
onto the dance floor and
started dancing, keeping a
safe distance from the
clumsy teachers. Then a
few others joined them,
followed by some boys. It
seemed like the teachers'

awful dancing had given everyone else a
bit of confidence. In just a few minutes,
the empty dance floor was packed.

"Should we dance, too?" Rachel asked,
turning to Kirsty.

But Kirsty looked alarmed as she stared
at the dancers. "It's getting
dangerous out there, if
you ask me!" she
replied. "Look!"
Rachel turned
back to see that it
wasn't just the
teachers who were
dancing badly now.
Nobody could dance well at all! As
Rachel watched, she saw one girl lose
her balance and crash into her friend.
Then, on the other side of the room, she

saw a boy fall over, dragging a couple of guys down with him.

"I've never seen such horrible dancing," Rachel whispered to Kirsty in dismay. "Someone's going to get hurt pretty soon!"

Kirsty nodded. "We really need to find the ribbon," she whispered back, "before

this turns into a total disaster! Come on, let's start looking."

Rachel scanned the room, wondering where they should begin their search. Her gaze fell upon a dancer in the far corner. He was short, dressed in white flared pants and high platform shoes. A huge pair of sunglasses hid most of his face. "Ooh," she said to Kirsty, pointing at the dancer. "*He* has good moves, doesn't he?"

Kirsty watched the boy. "Yes, he does," she agreed. "How strange that he's such a good

dancer, when everyone else is so terrible."

Rachel frowned. "Actually, the people who are dancing near him aren't that bad, either," she said.

The girls stared at the boy as he whirled around the dance floor.

"I don't recognize him," Kirsty said after a minute or two. "I'm sure I haven't seen him at school before. I wonder if he's someone's little brother."

Just then, the song ended and the girls edged forward, trying to get

a better look at the dancing boy as he came to a stop.

Kirsty frowned. He had unusually pointy ears, and even though the flashing disco lights were making everyone's faces turn funny colors, she was sure she could see a greenish tint to his skin. . . .

"Rachel!" Kirsty gulped. "I think that boy is really a *goblin*! Look at his ears!"

Rachel gazed across the dance floor. "You're right!" she exclaimed. "He must be the goblin with the disco ribbon! *That's* why he's such a good dancer."

Kirsty nodded. Her eyes were fixed on the goblin who was now dancing to the

next song, bouncing to the beat on his
gigantic platform shoes. "And that's why
everyone near him is dancing well," she
added. "The disco ribbon's magic
is affecting them, too!"

"Let's try and get
closer," Rachel
suggested, "and see
if we can spot the
magic ribbon."

Kirsty agreed. "We
might even be able to
grab it without him
noticing, once we know where the
ribbon is. He's totally wrapped up in the
music."

The girls made their way across the
dance floor, dodging the wacky dancing

that was going on around them. It didn't get any easier as they moved closer to the goblin. A crowd had gathered around him, and everyone was trying to copy his disco moves.

"I thought Jack Frost told his goblins that they had to stay *hidden* while they had the ribbons," Kirsty said to Rachel over the thumping music. "He certainly isn't hiding." Rachel laughed. "But he is in disguise," she added, swerving to avoid a boy who had just managed to trip over his own feet. "*Ow!*" She

gasped as somebody else barged right into her, knocking her to the floor.

Kirsty bent down to help her friend up. When the girls were both standing again, they realized that something terrible had happened: the goblin had vanished!

Goblin Goes Missing

"Oh no!" said Rachel, frantically looking around. "Where is he?"

"I can't see him anywhere," Kirsty replied. "But look, the people who were near him are dancing badly now, just like everyone else. He must be gone."

Rachel suddenly spotted something strange. "Hey," she said. "Look at that

mirror ball up there, Kirsty. Is it my
imagination, or is it shimmering more
brightly than the others?"

She and Kirsty gazed up at the mirror
ball — and then jumped with surprise as
a tiny fairy darted out from behind it in a
cloud of green sparkles.

"It's Jade the Disco Fairy!" Kirsty cried.

The girls shielded their eyes from the
bright lights as Jade waved at them and
fluttered down to land on
Kirsty's shoulder.
Luckily, everyone else
was so busy dancing
badly and bumping
into one another
that they didn't
notice the tiny
fairy!

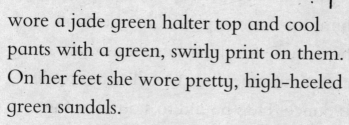

Jade had long
blond hair. She
wore a jade green halter top and cool
pants with a green, swirly print on them.
On her feet she wore pretty, high-heeled
green sandals.

"Hello, Jade," Rachel said as they
moved to the side of the dance floor

where it was a little quieter. "Did you see the goblin?"

"I certainly did," Jade said, rolling her eyes. "And I've never seen such a terrible outfit! It's enough to give disco a bad name! Those shoes — I mean, really!"

Kirsty laughed. "Did you see where he went?" she asked. "We lost him."

Jade shook her head. "I lost track of him, too," she replied, "but he can't have gone far. If he has my ribbon, I can guarantee that all he'll want to do is dance! He's bound to stay near the music."

"Well, he's not in the gym anymore," Rachel said. "But maybe he's close."

"Let's go out into the hallway," Kirsty suggested, walking toward a nearby door. "We can start looking there."

The girls and Jade went out the door. It was cooler and quieter in the hallway, though they could still hear the beat of the music from the disco. They hurried along the hall, looking into the classrooms they passed.

The first two rooms were empty, but as Kirsty popped her

head around the door of the third, she smiled. The goblin was dancing on top of the desks and singing really badly to the disco music!

She drew her head back quickly before he spotted her. "He's in there!" she whispered to Rachel and Jade. "What should we do?"

"Do?" Jade replied. "We'll go right in there and ask for my ribbon back, that's what we'll do! Come on!"

Ribbon In Reach

Jade zipped into the classroom, with Rachel and Kirsty right behind her. The goblin was now dancing on a desk right under a solar system mobile that dangled from the ceiling. He was having a great time, shimmying along to the music, his big high shoes

banging loudly on the desktop with
every step.

Jade fluttered over to him, and the girls
gathered by his desk.

"I believe you've got my disco ribbon,"
Jade said. "And I'd like it back now,
thank you very much!"

At her words, the
goblin pushed his huge
sunglasses off his
face and almost
fell off the desk
in surprise.

"Go away!
Can't you see I'm
dancing?" he asked
rudely, flicking his sunglasses
down onto his nose again, and turning
his back on the three friends.

Rachel watched him strutting his stuff. "I hate to say this, but he's actually very good," she said in a low voice.

"I can't believe he can dance like that in those huge platforms!" Kirsty agreed.

Jade didn't look so impressed. "Hmmmph!" she sniffed angrily. "He doesn't have anything to do with it. It's all my ribbon's magic. He couldn't do the Hokey Pokey without that ribbon!"

The goblin danced around, clapping his hands in time to the music.

As he whirled around to face the girls again, he looked annoyed to see that they were still there.

Then a sly smirk appeared on his face.
"Hey, why don't you come and join me?"
he suggested. "I could teach you my
disco routine!"

Kirsty and Rachel shook their heads,
backing away. "No way," Rachel

replied. "We know you just
want to freeze us!"
"And we're not
going to fall for any
of your tricks,"
Kirsty told him.
The goblin
gave a cackle.
"Well, you're not

getting this ribbon back!" he said, pulling
a length of sparkly green ribbon out
of his pocket. "Maybe I'll freeze you
anyway, just for the fun of it!"

He made a leap
toward the girls, but
Jade quickly waved
her wand and
turned them into
fairies, so that they
could zoom out of
his way.

Kirsty grinned as
she flapped her delicate wings
and fluttered out of the goblin's reach.
Being able to fly was so much fun — and
useful, too!

The three fairies circled the goblin's
head as he glared at them. "Leave me
alone!" he growled, climbing back onto
the desk. "Can't a goblin dance in
peace?"

"Not with my ribbon, you can't," Jade

insisted. "Now hand it over, or we'll buzz around your head like annoying mosquitoes until you do!"

"Then I'll have to *swat* you like mosquitoes!" snarled the goblin, making another leap for them. He held his big hands flat like flyswatters. As he did, the sparkly green disco ribbon flew out from

between his fingers and looped around
the model of Saturn on the solar system
mobile above his head.

The goblin reached up and tugged at
it, but the ribbon was caught on Saturn's
rings and wouldn't budge. "Silly thing!"
The goblin moaned,
jumping up and down
and yanking at it
with all his might.

The solar system
mobile swung back
and forth, but the
ribbon held fast.

Jade's eyes lit up. "This
could be our chance to get my
ribbon back!" she said to Rachel and
Kirsty in a low voice. "How can we get
the goblin to let go of the other end?"

Kirsty grinned. "Tickle him!" she suggested.

On previous fairy adventures, she and Rachel had discovered that the goblins were *extremely* ticklish.

Jade chuckled. "That's a fabulous idea," she said. "I'll tickle the goblin with my wand, and you two can fly to the mobile and untangle the ribbon while he's distracted."

"Let's do it!" Rachel said eagerly. Jade murmured some magic words. Her wand suddenly grew much longer and sprouted a super-tickly, feathery tip! "There," she said with a smile. "Let's see if this does the trick."

She flew down toward the goblin and poked the feathery wand under his arm as he pulled on the ribbon.

He immediately shrieked with laughter
and lowered his arm. "Ooh! Ooh! Stop
it!" he yelped, still holding onto the
ribbon and making the planets on the
mobile crash together above his head.

Jade didn't stop. She wiggled the wand
under his chin next, and the goblin
collapsed in giggles.

"Ooh, no! No!" he cackled. "Stop!"

But the little fairy was a blur. She flew

all around the goblin, tickling him on the
backs of his knees and behind his big ears
until he was helpless with laughter. The
girls watched as the goblin's grip on the
ribbon began to slip.

Kirsty and Rachel flew up to the
mobile and began trying to untangle the
ribbon from Saturn's rings. By now, the
goblin was laughing uncontrollably. His
sunglasses flew off because his whole
body was shaking with giggles! The
goblin dropped to his knees, squirming
and laughing, and then, to the girls'
delight, he dropped the end of the
disco ribbon.

Bowled Over

"It worked!" Kirsty whispered excitedly, gazing at the dangling ribbon. "Quick, Rachel, we just have to untie this end and we'll have it!"

"There!" Rachel cried, as the tangled end of the ribbon came free. She reached out to grab it, but before she could get a proper grip, the ribbon slipped right

through her fingers and fell onto the goblin's head!

"Oh no!" Rachel cried, swooping down to try and retrieve the ribbon.

The goblin, feeling the soft ribbon land on his head, was so surprised that he stopped laughing. Then he realized what had happened. With a look of glee on his face, he grabbed the ribbon, stuffed it into his pants pocket, and jumped down from the desk. "Can't catch me!" he yelled. Sticking his tongue out rudely at the three girls, he ran straight out of the classroom. Jade shook her wand,

turning it back to normal at once. "After him!" she cried.

Jade, Kirsty, and Rachel flapped their wings hard, zoomed across the classroom, and soared back into the hallway after the goblin.

Kirsty noticed that the goblin was having a hard time running in his platform shoes. He was very wobbly and stumbled a few times, but he still managed to stay ahead of the girls.

"Why is he so wobbly?" Kirsty asked Jade. "I thought the ribbon helped him keep his balance, even with those humongous shoes."

"It does," Jade replied. "Just as long as he's disco dancing." She grinned. "But now that he's running instead of dancing, the ribbon's magic doesn't help."

Rachel, Kirsty, and Jade flapped their wings even harder, but they weren't catching up to the goblin.

"We can't let him get away!" Rachel cried.

The goblin ran past a door that led

into the gym, and the three fairies
raced after him. As they passed the
open door, one of the sparkly disco
balls caught Kirsty's eye — and
then a brilliant idea popped into
her head!

"Jade," she called quickly, "do you
think you could use your magic to make
a big mirror ball like the ones hanging
from the ceiling in the gym?"

Jade frowned. "Yes, of course," she said. "But why?"

"There's no time to explain," Kirsty said, "but could you make one appear, please, and turn me and Rachel back into girls, too?"

"Sure," Jade replied, looking confused. She stopped flying and waved her wand over Kirsty and Rachel. With a flurry of green sparkles, the girls' wings

disappeared, and they were normal girls again. Jade waved her wand a second time and a stream of green fairy dust swirled

toward Kirsty. Instantly, a sparkly green mirror ball appeared in Kirsty's arms.

"He's getting away!" Rachel called urgently, as the goblin got closer to the end of the hallway.

"Yes, but not for long, if you can bowl another strike!" Kirsty said, shoving the mirror ball into Rachel's hands. "Go ahead, Rachel! Bowl that goblin over!"

Disco Divas

Rachel laughed as she realized what Kirsty had in mind. "I'll do my best," she said, bending down. Keeping her eye on the running goblin, she took careful aim and bowled the mirror ball.

Whoosh! Along the hallway it rolled, perfectly straight, heading directly for the

goblin. *CRASH!* It whacked right into
the goblin's platform shoes and sent him
flying!

"STRIKE!" Rachel, Kirsty, and Jade
cheered, hurrying down the hall to where
the goblin lay sprawled on the floor.

"Great bowling, Rachel!" Jade
declared.

"Thanks," Rachel said with a grin. "Now where's the disco ribbon?"

As the girls arrived, the goblin was desperately trying to get to his feet. But he couldn't catch his balance as he tried to stand in his huge platform shoes.

Thump! Down he went again. This time, the ribbon spilled out of his pocket.

Kirsty rushed forward and
grabbed it before the
goblin could even
think about using his
freezing magic on her.

"Thanks, Mr. Goblin,"
she said, cleverly ducking
out of the goblin's way.

The goblin kicked off his platform
shoes in a rage and got to his feet,
rubbing his hip where he'd fallen on it.
He scowled at the girls.

"Dumb shoes! I would have
gotten away if it hadn't
been for *them*!" he
complained. He stomped
off without another
word, his big green feet
slapping against the floor.

"Here you go, Jade," Kirsty said proudly, holding the disco ribbon up to the little fairy.

Jade waved her wand and green sparkles swirled all over the ribbon, shrinking it back to its Fairyland size.

"Thank you, girls," Jade said, smiling as she reattached the ribbon to the end of her wand. A burst of sparkles surrounded the wand and the ribbon as they came together, and the ribbon seemed to glow an even deeper green.

"That's more like it," Jade said,

twirling her wand with a smile on her face. "Disco divas everywhere will move and groove a whole lot better now!"

"Great," Rachel said, beaming. "No more stepping on toes at the school disco then, I hope!"

Jade shook her head. "Definitely not," she replied. "When you go back, you'll see that everyone is having a much better time in the gym."

"Hooray!" Kirsty said, and then she strained to listen as a new song started up. "Oh, I love this one!" she exclaimed, doing a little dance on the spot.

Jade grinned and kissed both girls.

"Thanks again," she said. "Now go and have some fun. I can see that Kirsty's dying to be a disco diva herself!"

"I'll do my best." Kirsty laughed. "Bye, Jade!"

"Bye," Rachel added, waving at the fairy. "Come on, Kirsty, let's hit the dance floor!"

Jade fluttered away down the hallway, leaving a trail of green sparkles in her wake. Then Kirsty and Rachel boogied their way back into the school gym. The dance floor was full, and everyone was having fun. But, best of all, nobody was falling over or bumping into each other anymore!

The two friends made their way onto the packed dance floor and joined in the dancing.

"I'm so glad we helped find the disco ribbon," Rachel called over to Kirsty with a grin. "This is so much fun!"

Kirsty nodded. "I know," she replied. Then she looked up and saw that there was a new mirror ball hanging from the ceiling — an extra-sparkly, *green* mirror

ball that sent thousands of jade-green
lights whirling around the room with
every spin.

"I love helping the fairies," Kirsty said
to Rachel, pointing out the mirror ball
with a grin. "And I can't wait to find
another one of the dance ribbons!"

THE DANCE FAIRIES

Jade the Disco Fairy has
her magic ribbon back. Now Rachel
and Kirsty must help

Rebecca
the Rock 'n' Roll
Fairy!

Join their next adventure in this special
sneak peek!

Rock 'n' Roll Party

"Are you ready yet, Mom?" Kirsty Tate called up the stairs. "Rachel and I are dying to see your costumes!" She grinned over at her best friend, Rachel Walker, who was standing next to her.

"We'll be down soon," Mrs. Tate called back from the bedroom.

Kirsty and Rachel sat down on the bottom stair to wait.

"I *wish* we were going to the rock 'n' roll party with my mom and dad." Kirsty sighed. "It sounds like fun, *and* we might find Rebecca the Rock 'n' Roll Fairy's magic ribbon there!"

Rachel nodded. "The Dance Fairies are depending on us!" she reminded Kirsty.

"We've gotten a good start," Kirsty remarked. "We already found Bethany the Ballet Fairy's ribbon, and Jade the Disco Fairy's, too."

"But if we don't find the rest, all the other kinds of dancing will keep on going wrong, and dancing won't be fun any more!" Rachel sighed.

"Yes, and I guess the dancing at the rock 'n' roll party tonight will be ruined since Rebecca's rock 'n' roll ribbon is still missing," Kirsty replied with a worried frown.

"Girls, we're ready!" Mr. Tate yelled from upstairs, and Kirsty and Rachel turned around.

Mr. and Mrs. Tate came downstairs, and the girls' eyes widened with delight.

Kirsty's dad was wearing jeans and a black leather jacket. Kirsty's mom was wearing a sleeveless black top and a full white skirt embroidered with black musical notes. She wore a high ponytail tied with a red ribbon.

"You both look *fantastic*!" Kirsty gasped.

"You look like you just walked out of the movie *Grease*!" Rachel added. "Will everyone be dressed up like you?"

Mr. Tate nodded. "There will also be demonstrations of rock 'n' roll dancing," he explained, "and an Elvis impersonator. Elvis Presley was a famous rock 'n' roll singer, you know."

"And Kirsty's Uncle John is in charge of the music," Mrs. Tate told Rachel. "We're taking some of our own rock 'n' roll records for him to play."

"It sounds like fun," Kirsty said wistfully.

"Well, why don't you two come with us?" Mrs. Tate suggested with a smile. "We didn't ask you before because there aren't going to be any other kids there, but you might enjoy it."

Kirsty and Rachel looked thrilled.

"Can we?" Kirsty asked eagerly. "But what about Gran? She was going to come and stay with us."

"She won't have left home yet," Mrs. Tate said, glancing at the clock. "I'll give her a call."

"Does it matter that we don't have costumes?" Rachel asked.

"Not at all," Mr. Tate assured her.

"Isn't this great?" Kirsty whispered to Rachel as they went to grab their coats. "We're going to the rock 'n' roll party after all!"

"Yes, and maybe we'll find Rebecca's rock 'n' roll ribbon!" Rachel replied excitedly.

RAINBOW magic™

THE WEATHER FAIRIES

Rain or Shine, It's Fairy Time!

Come flutter by Butterfly Meadow

3 1901 04563 1860